My Bunkmate Hates Puppies

Written by **Sam Hay**

Illustrated by **Ria Maria Lee**

𝒟ISNEY • Hyperion

Los Angeles   New York

First Hardcover Edition, April 2023
First Paperback Edition, April 2023

10 9 8 7 6 5 4 3 2 1

FAC-004510-23069
Printed in the United States of America

This book is set in Aptifer Slab LT Pro/Linotype
Designed by Zareen Johnson
Illustrations created in Photoshop

Library of Congress Cataloging-in-Publication Data

Names: Hay, Sam, author.
Title: My bunkmate hates puppies / Sam Hay.
Description: First paperback edition. • Los Angeles : DisneyHyperion, [2023] • Series: Camp Lil' Vills ; Book 1 • Audience: Ages 6 to 8 • Audience: Grades 2–3 • Summary: At her father's summer camp set in the middle of an enchanted forest, Bloom finds herself bunking with Cruella de Vil, who hates puppies (and pretty much everything else), and who wants to steal the rare furry Nerbit and turn it into a fancy hat.
Identifiers: LCCN 2021042467 (print) • LCCN 2021042468 (ebook) • ISBN 9781368084420 (hardcover) • ISBN 9781368057400 (paperback) • ISBN 9781368074070 (ebk)
Subjects: LCSH: Magic—Juvenile fiction. • Animals, Mythical—Juvenile fiction. • Theft—Juvenile fiction. • CYAC: Magic—Fiction. • Camps—Fiction. • Animals, Mythical—Fiction. • Stealing—Fiction.
Classification: LCC PZ7.H31387385 My 2023 (print) • LCC PZ7.H31387385 (ebook) • DDC 813.6 [Fic]—dc23/eng/20220111
LC record available at https://lccn.loc.gov/2021042467
LC ebook record available at https://lccn.loc.gov/2021042468

Welcome to the Lilliputian Villages Summer Camp, where you'll learn everything from dragon care to spells and crafts.

We'll be making magical memories together, so there's no need to bring any enchanted equipment or pets from home. All tools will be provided.

And most importantly, all campers are welcome.

Your Camp Director,

Mr. Maj

(Yes, that Mr. Maj. Worry not—I use my magic strictly for good now. And for extra scorched s'mores.)

1

I poked my head out of the cabin door and looked around at the new campers arriving. There were giggly witches and wisecracking werewolves and fun fairy kids flapping their wings with excitement. *Which ones will be my new bunkmates? I wondered. Hopefully, whoever they are, they'll be a tiny bit tidier than the last lot. Broomsticks crossed!*

The girl who'd had the bed next to mine last week was a werewolf who liked to howl at the moon while rolling in mud. Her sheets got so caked in grime they made a rustling noise whenever she moved! And I didn't even want to think about the kid who had collected toadstools. She'd hoarded dozens of them in her socks—and mine! The cabin had stunk for days. And it was up to me to sort it all out.

I stepped back into the cabin and took the list of my new bunkmates' names out of my folder, pinning it neatly up on the cabin bulletin board. When my dad first opened Lilliputian Villages Summer Camp, I couldn't wait to get involved. The thought of spending my vacations in the middle of a magical forest made my spell-socks tingle! But I soon realized it wasn't all flying lessons and wild unicorn rides. There was so much to organize! See, while Dad's wonderful at wizardry (as a former "evil sorcerer" that's exactly what you'd expect), he's bottom of the class when it comes to planning. *So that's where I come in*, I reminded myself as I straightened a pillow. *Because I love making sure everything goes smoothly.*

"Oh, hi there." A fair-haired girl appeared in the doorway. "I think this is my cabin. . . ."

As soon as she walked inside, I spotted it. A strange-looking hairy banana sticking out of the top of her backpack! *Uh-oh! I know exactly what that is. . . .*

"I'm Hemlock," she added. "But my friends call me Hem. Do you know which bed is mine?"

"Um—hi," I said, trying to look at the list on the board, instead of staring at the banana, which had begun to twitch now. *Maybe I should warn her*, I thought. Because I knew exactly what was going to happen next. See, I'd tried that particular banana spell before, and it never lasted very—

POP!

"Oh!" Hem gasped as the banana suddenly turned back into a sandy-colored puppy. It leaped down from her backpack and began charging around our feet, barking and wagging its tail. "Buttons! Stop! Sit!" Hem said, trying to catch the pup.

I smiled. Okay, so maybe turning her dog into a banana so he could come to camp with her wasn't the best idea in the world. But I'd done the same thing when Dad first opened camp. I couldn't bear to leave my dog, Muffins, at home with Granny Maj, so I took him with me disguised as a banana. It had not gone well.

"Hush, Buttons!" Hem tried to hold him close to stop his barking. She glanced at me, her face tomato red. "He *really* wanted to come. I thought the spell would last longer."

"Same thing happened to me a few years ago," I said. "But my banana got muddled up with my bunkmate's picnic lunch. She got such a shock when we stopped for a snack, and my dog, Muffins, suddenly changed back!"

Hem giggled.

"I'm Bloom, by the way," I said, crouching

down to pet Buttons. "I like his collar. Purple's my favorite color."

"Mine, too," Hem said. "Do you think if Buttons is really good, he could stay?"

"Er—well . . ." I wasn't sure what to say because it was against camp rules:

No wishing stones. No wands. No broomsticks. And definitely no pets!

Though I kept a wand stashed away for emergencies (it seemed smart ever since one of my previous bunkmates turned my bed into a flying carpet), I kind of agreed with the pet thing. I missed Muffins a lot, but mucky puppies made the bunks super messy!

"Buttons, SIT!" Hem sighed. "I guess the spell's got him all excited. Magic does that to him. And look, his ears are still yellow."

"Aw, yellow ears are cool." I gave Buttons another tickle and he rewarded me with a big lick. "Don't worry," I told Hem. "It'll wear off after a few hours. At least it did with Muffins."

"Yuck!" said a loud voice behind us. "No, no, NO, Dahling!"

I looked around to find another new arrival— a small girl with black and white pigtails dressed in a smart fur cloak (I'm sure it wasn't real fur!). Behind her, she dragged a spotless, fancy trunk. The sparkly diamonds on it made my eyes blink.

Whoa! I thought. *She looks as though she pre-fers things clean, just like me!* I felt a sudden bud of hope in my belly. Had my wishes for at least one tidy bunkmate finally been answered?

The new girl scowled at Buttons. "What a dreadful creature! Dogs aren't allowed at camp. He's got to go!"

But Buttons had other ideas. He bounded over to her, woofing and wagging his tail.

"Buttons!" Hem shouted. "Stop right there!"

But Buttons didn't stop. He didn't even slow down.

Uh-oh! This is not going to end well.

I could barely watch as he charged toward her, his tongue dribbling, his ears flapping. The girl backed away, bumping into her trunk and knocking it over. And then he launched himself at her, ready to deliver a big, wet, sloppy, soggy-doggy hello.

2

"**EWW!**" the girl howled, slapping him away. "Horrible, filthy beast!"

Hem grabbed Buttons's collar and pulled him off. "I'm so sorry. He just wants to be your friend."

She wiped the drool off her face onto her cloak, then wagged her finger at Hem. "I'm going to report you!"

My tummy was churning now, like a spell-mixing machine on max power. As the camp owner's daughter, I always tried to help my bunkmates settle in and make friends—and now two of them were having a first-class, full-on, face-to-face falling-out! I racked my brains for a quick fix. *If only I knew the magic spell to turn Buttons into a unicorn*, I thought. *No one ever gets cross with a unicorn.* "Hi," I said to the new girl. "I'm Bloom. What's your name?"

The girl looked down her nose at me as though I were something squidgy she'd stepped in. "I'm Cruella," she said, tossing her pigtails. "Get that mangy mutt out of here, NOW!"

Buttons gave a bark and Cruella jumped back.

"Um—Hem, how about we go find a counselor," I said, stepping in between her and Cruella. "Maybe they could *magic* Buttons home for you; that's what Dad did when I brought my dog to camp. He turned him into a letter and sent him through the mail."

Hem nodded. "I guess that would be okay. I'll find his leash. . . ." She dropped her backpack on the floor and began rummaging inside.

Cruella, meanwhile, hauled her trunk toward her bed, sniffing the air and frowning. "Urgh! It smells just awful in here." She flipped open the trunk lid and pulled out a bottle of perfume and began squirting it around the cabin. Buttons let out a whimper. Hem held her nose, and I tried

not to cough as a cloud of flowery scent drifted around the room.

"Er—maybe that's enough now," I said, flipping open a window.

But Cruella had stopped spraying and had pulled out an expensive set of bedding. "The higher the thread count, the softer the sheet," she said, when she noticed me watching her. "And these," she added, rubbing her cheek against her linen, "are the best money can buy."

Whoa! I thought. *She really does like everything to be perfect. Maybe that's why she got a little cranky with Hem's dog.*

"Found it!" Hem said, holding up Buttons's leash. At the sight of it the little pup began leaping around, barking with joy.

"Quiet!" Cruella grabbed her perfume again. "One more bark and I'll zap him!"

Huh? That's a bit mean! "Um—maybe we should go now," I said, hurrying Hem and Buttons toward the door.

As we stepped outside, I felt the warm sun on my face, and saw the other new campers arriving at their bunks.

"This is such a cool place," Hem said, looking around at the different trail signposts. "Is there really an enchanted wood down there?"

"Yep, and there are real unicorns in Bluebell Dell, too. Sometimes they even let you pet them."

"Wow! Maybe I won't be homesick without Buttons after all," Hem said.

Homesick? A sudden thought stopped me in my tracks. *Maybe that's what's making Cruella a little cranky—she's missing home.* It was understandable. Everyone missed home sometimes. *And it's okay to be nervous about dogs, too,* I reminded myself. Everyone has something they're scared of. *I mean that whole "magic mirror on the wall" thing really creeps me out. Once Cruella settles in, we'll probably all be laughing our spell-socks off at the "soggy-doggy-face-wash incident."*

I linked my arm through Hem's. "Come on, let's go drop off Buttons with a counselor, then we'll pick up some blueberry sparkle muffins from the welcome stand. We'll take one back for Cruella, too." *I'm sure she'll be happy as an elf at Christmas, as soon as she settles in! (Broomsticks crossed!)*

3

UNFORTUNATELY, the whole muffins-make-things-better idea was a ten on the fail-o-meter.

"Now remember, *Bloop*," Cruella said as we walked down the path after everyone had unpacked. "I NEVER eat muffins! I only like French patisserie."

"Sure, no problem." I pretended I hadn't heard her get my name wrong AGAIN. So far, in the space of ten minutes, she had called me Broom, Balloon, Zoom, Doom, Gloom, and—my favorite— Varooooom! *But I guess it is hard to remember names when there are so many new people to get to know*, I told myself.

I glanced across at Cruella, who was walking on tiptoes down the path in her fancy red high-heeled boots—she seemed determined not to get them dirty. I'd offered her my spare pair of old sneakers, but she had turned her nose up at them. "And as for this," she had said, holding up the camp shirt we were all supposed to wear, "it's not even silk!"

Maybe Creature Care Class will make her smile, I thought. *She might not like dogs, but no one can resist a baby Pegasus or a fluffy griffin chick.*

Creature Care Class was my secret weapon when it came to helping bunkmates settle in. Being able to get up close to some of the rarest magical animals never failed to amaze even the crankiest kids.

"This is it," I said, leading Cruella and Hem and our other new bunkmates, up the steps into the activity center. But as I opened the door . . .

"Wait—we must be in the wrong place," I said. For starters there were no creatures. Just piles of old trash lying on the tables—a broken umbrella, a basket of odd socks, a single smelly sneaker with no laces. There was no teacher, either. *Where's Dad?* I looked at the clock. He wasn't usually late.

"What a mess!" Cruella picked up a dusty ball of yarn and wrinkled her nose.

"Perhaps we should tidy it all up," I said.

The kids who had arrived before us seemed restless. A few were wandering around the room. Others were throwing some old tennis balls they'd found at each other. One looked like she was about to leave!

Uh-oh! If Dad doesn't hurry up, I'll have to teach the class. I was just wondering if I could remember the make-a-dragon spell off the top of my head, when Cruella gave a squeal.

"Eww!" she said, picking up an old tin can. "This smells dreadful!"

A small boy stepped forward. "Um—old tin cans are actually very useful." He peered at Cruella through thick glasses. "If you're camping, you can use a tin can to mix up a potion." As he spoke, his glasses changed color from purple to a lizard green.

"Wow, are your glasses enchanted?" I asked him.

His face turned red and so did his glasses. He smiled at me. "Um—yeah—I put a chameleon spell on them."

"Cool!" I said. "I'm Bloom, by the way. What's your name?"

"Benji," he said. "Want me to show you what else my glasses can do? See, if I want to look at something really close up," he said, picking up the tin can, "then I just need to think 'microscope,' and this happens—"

The lenses of his glasses popped out, changing into long, narrow eyepieces.

"Whoa," I breathed. "That's so neat!"

Benji peered into the tin can. "Ooh, there are amazing bugs inside."

Cruella shuddered. "Disgusting!"

"No, it's actually quite incredible," Benji said. "See, the bugs are eating up all the tiny bits of food left inside, like little recycle machines. You should see."

"Not a chance, Dahling!" Cruella turned her back on him and folded her arms.

"I'll look," I said, taking the glasses. "Oh yeah, I can see the bugs wriggling at the bottom." I frowned. I liked minibeasts, but I preferred them outside. "Um—maybe we should let them go. There's a log pile by the door." *Then we can clean up the rest of this trash*. I kind of agreed with Cruella about how messy it all looked lying around the classroom.

But the other kids were crowding around us now, all wanting to see the bugs through Benji's glasses. As I handed the tin can to Hem, it began to shake.

"Ow!" Hem gasped, dropping it on the table. "It's hot!"

Yellow smoke was coming out of it, too. And it had begun to twitch and tap up and down.

Uh-oh! Something weird is happening here. "Um—maybe step back everyone," I said. "It looks like it's about to—"

4

BANG!

Cruella screamed. Benji sneezed. Everyone ducked!

Through the smoke I could see a dark shape looming.

"Dad!" I yelled.

"Wizarding wands!" Benji breathed.

I felt a bubble of pride in my tummy. No one could do spells like my dad.

"Welcome to Creature Care Class," Dad said, stepping out of the smoke. "My name is Mr. Maj, and I wanted to show you that with magical creatures, you must always expect the unexpected." As he spoke, the piles of trash that were lying on the tables around the room began to change.

The basket of old socks turned into a litter of tiny snapdragons. The sneaker changed into a baby Pegasus. The umbrella was actually a

griffin. The tennis balls became tufted toad-lings. And the old yarn changed into a—

"Fuzzy-headed Nerbit!" Benji squealed. "Oh, my magical moons! I've never seen one of them before."

"A what?" Cruella peered at the bright orange creature that Benji was pointing to.

"A Fuzzy-headed Nerbit!" Benji said again. "Can you believe it?"

"What an ugly little lump," Cruella said, wrinkling her nose. "And such a vile color! Haven't you got any pandas? Or penguins? Or at least a zebra or two? Their skins are much more my cup of tea."

"Shh," I whispered to her. "Nerbits are very sensitive. They can understand everything we say."

As if in reply the Nerbit shrank back from Cruella and hid its face with its trunk.

"And they're rare!" Benji said. "Look, I'll show you." He reached into his pocket and pulled out a bulging wallet full of cards. "I've been collecting *Awesome Creature* trading cards since I was four—they tell you everything you'll ever need to know about amazing animals." He began flicking through them until— "Here it is...." He dangled a card under Cruella's nose. "See— Fuzzy-headed Nerbit. Rarity factor one hundred."

But Cruella wasn't looking at the card. She was staring at the Nerbit. "Rare, you say? And such a silky, long, and unusually fluffy coat."

"Yes, and did you know the Nerbit's toes are made of real gold?" Benji said. "When they walk, their feet sort of shine."

Cruella's eyes grew wider. "Golden toes? I LOVE gold," she purred.

Huh? Cruella suddenly seemed *really* interested in the Nerbit. Was she hoping to take it home for a pet? Dad would never let that happen. "Let's go meet the snapdragons," I said, stepping in between her and the fuzzy creature. "They're cool, too, aren't they, Benji?" I said, hoping he'd change the subject.

"Oh sure, snapdragons are awesome," he said. "But the Nerbit . . . I mean, wow!" He looked at his card again. "It says here, there are only four Nerbits left in the world."

Cruella snatched the card out of Benji's hand. "What? It's almost extinct? How simply wonderful!" She gave an odd little cackle, then—"You!" she said, poking Benji. "Come and tell me EVERYTHING you know about it!"

5

I couldn't take my eyes off Cruella. Even though I was supposed to be polishing the baby griffin's claws, which is one of my favorite jobs at Creature Care Class, I watched her quiz Benji about the Nerbit. She'd taken a bright red notebook out of her bag now, and was writing in it using a long, thin black pen. Every so often she'd use the pen to point at the Nerbit, or to poke Benji with, when he stopped talking for a moment to take a breath.

Usually, it's the baby Pegasus that gets everyone excited. I glanced over to the flying horse's table, and sure enough, Hem and a little group of campers were brushing its silver tail and stroking its wings. I was pleased to see that Hem looked happy and didn't appear to be missing her dog. (Just as I'd suggested, a counselor had mailed Buttons safely home.) But Cruella was a bit of a worry; though I'd wanted her to settle into camp life, something just didn't seem right about her sudden interest in the Nerbit. I was just about to go over to her, when my dad suddenly clapped his hands.

"Attention, everyone," he said. "Please come and take a wand from this box. It is time for spelling practice."

Cruella scowled, but Benji was already running to grab a wand, so she snapped her red notebook shut and pushed the pen behind her ear.

Dad waited until everyone was quiet, and then he began, "One of the best ways to learn about magical creatures is to become one! You can't understand an animal until you've walked in its hooves, paws, fins, or what-have-you. Now, I want you all to get into pairs. I'm going to teach you a mirror spell, so you can turn each other into magical creatures at the same time."

There were shouts of delight. Benji hopped from foot to foot, his eyes as wide as his smile. I felt a bubble of excitement, too. Mirror spells were always fun. The double dose of magic made the results much more effective.

The only person who wasn't smiling was Cruella. "I'm not doing it!" she said. "Magic gives me a migraine. And besides"—she plucked her pen out from behind her ear and pointed it at the rest of us—"who knows what sort of ghastly creature you lot might turn me into."

"That's quite all right," my dad said in his most soothing voice. "You can just watch."

See, Dad always tries to make every camper feel comfortable, even the cranky ones. He says it's because he knows what it's like to be a little different. As a former evil sorcerer, Dad used to live in a creepy old castle and unleash lightning bolts and bad spells on anyone who annoyed him. Then I came along, and he changed. He turned his lightning bolts into fairy lights for my nursery and used his magic to make the most amazing toys for me, like flying tricycles and real live teddy bears. But even when he stopped being an evil sorcerer, some people were still scared of him. So he always says he wants camp to feel like a safe space to everyone—especially those who are misunderstood.

"Perhaps you might like to make some notes in your journal?" Dad suggested to Cruella now.

Cruella hugged the book tightly to her chest. "Maybe I will. Maybe I won't."

Benji tapped me on the shoulder. "Um—can I be your partner, please?" He pushed his glasses up his nose. "I love doing spells, but magic makes me sneeze, and sometimes things go a little wonky."

"Er, sure—no problem." I crossed my fingers

behind my back and hoped his spell wouldn't go wrong today. Not like last week, when another camper turned me into a goldfish but forgot the tank of water! Luckily, Dad turned me back before I ran out of air.

Dad swept over to the blackboard, his dark cloak billowing behind. "Gather round and I'll show you the magic words you're going to say." He held his hand in the air, and a piece of chalk appeared between his fingers. Then he leaned in and began writing some words. His large, loopy letters wriggled and jiggled on the board for a moment as they settled in place.

Dibble, Dabble, Fur and Claw, he wrote.

Transform this person, tail to paw.

"Now, remember, as you say the words," Dad explained, "make a large figure eight with your wand over your partner's head and think of the creature you want them to become. But don't tell them exactly what you're planning. Make it a surprise!" He smiled. "Oh, and be sure to give yourselves plenty of space. Magic can be messy."

"Exactly!" Cruella said. "That's why magic is for fools." She stalked back to the Nerbit's table and began making notes again.

I really wanted to go and convince her to join the group. But Benji was already practicing the magic words under his breath in front of me. "I've got so many great ideas of what to change you into," he said. "I'm thinking of something spectacular, really big, with horns—wait—" He frowned. "Was it a figure eight or a circle we make with the wand?"

"A figure eight," I said nervously. I liked Benji, and he seemed to know a lot about magical things. But he also looked a little unsure.

"Got it!" Benji grinned. "Let's get started." And he lifted his wand high into the air.

I tried to smile back, but my tummy felt like it was full of jelly snakes, all slithery and squishy. I took a deep breath. *Broomsticks crossed this is going to be okay*, I thought as I raised my wand.

As soon as Benji started to say the magic words, he sneezed. And suddenly I was falling.

Whoa! Not falling. Shrinking! It was like the air was being sucked out of me by a giant vacuum cleaner. "Wahhh!" I yelled, or would have, if my voice hadn't shrunk, too, turning into a tiny little squeak as I hit the floor with a bump!

Uh-oh! I don't think this is quite what Benji had in mind, I thought, as I looked down at my six skinny little legs and my hard shell of a tummy. *I guess I'm some sort of bug, an ant maybe?* The

weird thing was, my brain didn't seem to have changed. *Didn't Dad say this spell was supposed to make you think like a creature? I don't seem to be having any buggy thoughts.*

I scratched my head with one of my feelers. *Maybe the spell went wrong when Benji sneezed—* "Hey! Watch it!" I yelped, as a giant pair of feet shuffled backward and nearly stood on me. *If I don't find somewhere to hide, I'm going to get squished!*

Across the floor, I could see a large shiny dome. *A pencil sharpener maybe? Perfect! I'll crawl inside until the magic wears off.* I set off, scuttling toward it. But moving six legs at the same time is *hard*, especially when you're dodging crumbs the size of boulders! *Yuck!* I puffed out my buggy cheeks. *I have to sweep the room when I get back to normal; this floor is disgusting!*

I'd just about reached the sharpener when— *THUMP!* A gigantic red boot heel crashed down in front of me. "EEK!" I swerved and smacked into one of the huge crumbs. *Urgh!* The squidgy, stale cookie crumb was sticking to my legs. But there was no time to shake it off—the giant red boot was moving again. It rose above my head, casting a huge dark shadow. "Hey! Don't squish me!" I yelled, waggling my legs and feelers. But the owner of the red boot obviously couldn't hear.

Ahhh! I closed my eyes and prepared to be pancaked.

6

JUST in time, I felt a rush of air, as I exploded upward, zooming toward the ceiling. And with a jolt, I was back to myself again.

"Oh, wow! You nearly got trampled!" Hem said. "If your dad hadn't reversed that spell, Cruella would have pulverized you."

"It's not my fault," Cruella muttered. "I didn't know that dreadful little ant was you, er—Moon? Raccoon? Platoon?" She pointed her long, thin black pen at me. "Just so you know: I DETEST bugs!"

I blinked. *Had she really been about to squash me* on purpose? I was about to tell her that whatever you think of bugs you should never hurt one, when I saw my dad looking at me. *Be kind,* I heard his voice in my head. That's one of Dad's slightly annoying magical skills. He can send thoughts without opening his mouth. I looked back at him and frowned. Before I could say anything, though, I felt a peck on my leg, and I looked down to find a little black-and-white creature tottering about. It honked and growled and flapped its flipper-claws and spun around a few times.

"Oh, my goodness," Hem said. "Is that a penguin-bear? It's adorable."

I felt a puff of pride in my chest then and smiled. "Um—yeah, that's what I turned Benji into."

Benji, the penguin-bear, honked again, then dived onto his belly and slid across the floor as though he were on an ice slide, scattering lots of unusual creatures out of the way.

"Wow," I said, gazing around the room. "There sure are some amazing animals in here." Behind us was a long-legged, fire-breathing flamingo, which was being chased by a baby mammoth. Two dragon-cats were wrestling on the floor in the corner, while perched on the light above us was a bizarre-looking beast—part panther and part parakeet, maybe?

Hem giggled. "Me and my partner didn't get the spell completely right." She held up one of her arms, which was shaped like a huge lobster claw. She pointed to a boy across the room, who was staring down at his giant duck feet. "I guess we both need a bit more practice."

"Don't worry," my dad said. "You will have lots of opportunity to test out your magical skills. And remember, taking risks is important. A little bit of danger keeps us all on our toes," he added, winking at me. "Now it's time for lunch, so I'd better return you all back to your former selves." He clicked his fingers and there was a loud *POP* as the campers snapped back into their usual forms.

"Oh, my word!" Benji shouted. "Did you see what you turned me into, Bloom? A penguin-bear! I can't wait to tell Mom. Oh, and hey! Did you like what I turned you into? A silver-tongued antelope is so cool, right?"

I guess he had no idea he'd turned me into an ant. "Um—sure," I said. "Shall we go eat lunch now?"

✦

Everyone from Creature Care Class sat outside the Cozy Cauldron Café on picnic tables. Benji, Hem, and the three other girls from our bunk—a smiley witch called Thursday, and two fairylike sisters named Blush and Luna—were talking about the activities they wanted to try. Two boys from Benji's bunk, a werewolf named Arthur and an elf called Colin, were levitating their milk cartons. I tried not to notice as they spilled milk all over the table.

Cruella didn't join in. She was still making notes in her journal, stopping every so often to pick up the silver fork and knife she'd brought with her to eat her sandwich. There wasn't a single crumb around her.

"So, you like journaling?" I said, trying to bring Cruella into the conversation.

She shrugged. "Where does the Nerbit sleep?"

"Um—in the Big Barn," I said. "You know, that red building near our cabin?"

Cruella snorted. "The Big Barn is minuscule!"

"Oh, but that's the magical part," Benji interrupted. "I read about it. See, it appears small on the outside but inside it's humongous—the size of at least a hundred football fields!"

Cruella rolled her eyes. "Impossible!"

"It's true," I said, impressed that Benji had done so much research about camp. "That's what makes Lilliputian Villages special. There are mysteries. And puzzles. And lots of magic. I'm always discovering new things...."

"Ooh, yes," Benji said, bouncing in his seat. "There are so many legends about this place. Some say there's a ghostly pirate ship in the lake. Others tell of a real live volcano beneath the camp. It could erupt at any moment!" His glasses were steaming up now. "And then I read this awesome book that said there are secret time

tunnels running all over camp, right underneath our feet. . . ."

I blinked at him. *Secret tunnels under our feet? I'd never heard of that before!*

"Yes, yes, but who cares about ships or volcanoes or stupid tunnels," Cruella interrupted. "I want to know more about the Big Barn. Why do the creatures need loads of space? Surely they live in small cages?"

"They're not kept in cages," I said.

Benji nodded. "You see, all the animals in the Big Barn have their own special wild habitats in the barn." His glasses began to glow as he got more excited. "Some of them, like the dragons, like to fly around at night and nest in rocky boulders. Others, like the Nerbit, prefer a snug, cozy cave to hide in. Oh, and then they need to have the right food. According to my *Awesome Creature* trading cards, the Nerbit mostly eats giggle-berries and buttercups. It's the buttercups that make its toes golden."

"Which is why the keepers grow a buttercup meadow in the Big Barn." I smiled at Benji. "Just for the Nerbit."

Cruella's eyes sparkled. "A buttercup meadow? I want to see that! Show me!"

I coughed. "Er—sorry, campers aren't allowed in the barn. The creatures are so special the keepers need to make sure they're safe and calm." There was still something unsettling about Cruella's interest in the Nerbit that I couldn't quite put my finger on, and I was glad the Big Barn wasn't open to visitors.

"Bloom's right," Benji said. "Which is why I've signed up for the Keepers' Care Club! I'm going to be allowed to help prepare the animals' food tonight, and the keepers have even told me their special secret spell-lock for the door." He dropped his voice to a whisper. "To open the barn, you just say the magic words:

"*'Ittle bittle, tick and tock,*
Magic key, this door unlock!'"

"Benji!" I gasped. "I'm sure you're not supposed to tell people that."

"Oops!" Benji's face—and glasses—turned beetroot red. "I'm sorry." He looked at Cruella. "You won't tell, will you?"

"Of course not!" She smiled at him. "Your secret is safe with me."

"Hey, how about we go to Crafty Corner after lunch?" I jumped in. "Last week, we made these amazing springy spell-socks that make you bounce super high!" *And best of all, Crafty Corner is on the other side of the camp,* I thought. *Far away from the Big Barn—and the Nerbit!*

THE walk over to Crafty Corner was one of my favorite routes in camp, mostly because you have to go through the Enchanted Woods. I love the way the smiley trees waggle their branches, and how the singing flowers change color depending on what song they're crooning. And best of all are the jelly-beanstalks that grow all along the path.

"Pick some, they're delicious," I told Hem, Benji, and Cruella.

"Oh, yum!" Hem said, grabbing a couple of jellybeans and popping them into her mouth. "Ooh, they taste of grapefruit—no—I mean raspberry. Actually, this one is more like strawberry milk?"

I laughed. "That's the surprise! You never know what flavor you'll get."

"Oh, I can help with that." Benji pushed his glasses up his nose and peered closely at the jelly-beanstalks. "See, I have this special mode on my lenses that can identify anything. Yep, they say that one there is pineapple flavor," he added, pointing to a bean. "And that one is chocolate—"

"I adore chocolate!" Cruella barged past him and tugged the jellybean off the stalk. But soon her smug smile disappeared. "Yuk! This is NOT chocolate! It doesn't taste anything like Belgian truffles."

"Um—maybe try another one," I suggested.

"This one!" Benji said, his face turning pink. He plucked another bean off the stalk and held it out to her. "My glasses say it's toffee!"

Cruella took it from him. But as she chewed, her eyes widened. "Urgh! It's not toffee, it's COFFEE!" She shuddered. "I only like tea! And it must be Earl Grey, with lemon, not milk. Now I feel sick!"

Uh-oh. Quick, Bloom! I told myself. *Distract her!* The last thing I wanted was a camper to get sick; I was supposed to be looking after them, not making them unwell.

"Hey, look," I said, pointing off into the trees. "Check out the Glow-Cart!"

A little go-cart covered in tiny twinkling lights whizzed past. Behind the wheel was one of the counselors. He waved as he went by.

"What on earth . . ." Cruella gasped.

"Oh, wow!" Benji breathed. "I wish I'd gotten a picture."

"Don't worry, you'll see loads," I said. "The counselors use them to get around."

"That's so cool," Hem said. "I've never seen anything so sparkly!"

Benji nodded. "That's because they're powered by fairy dust, according to the brochure."

Cruella's eyes narrowed. "I want to drive a Glow-Cart! Arrange it, NOW!"

"Sorry," I said. "Campers aren't allowed in them. They're way too fast."

"What? That's ridiculous!" Cruella flashed a glare at me. "I'm an excellent driver!"

"Oh, hey—look," I said, changing the subject. "Crafty Corner's just up there; how about we jog the rest of the way?"

I didn't dare look at Cruella's cranky face as we ran up the path toward the craft center. But as we got closer, I spotted Glissando, one of my favorite counselors, through the window, and I felt a wave of relief through my bones. Spending time with Glissando was a bit like swimming in the cool waters of the Moon Ponds. She had a way of making everyone feel calm. And she was really good at magic, too. She'd taught us spells for making delicious desserts during treat night last week.

"Hi, Bloom!" Glissando smiled as we walked into the hut. "And hi, everyone," she added to the others. "Come and see our exciting new laundry machine."

Cruella scowled. "I didn't come to camp to do laundry!"

"Oh no, no," Glissando said. "Let me explain. . . . It's an *enchanted* laundry machine." She pointed to a large shimmering square box on a table in the middle of the room, where a group of campers was already gathered. One of them was standing on a stool, pouring a bucket of what looked like leaves and branches

and moss into the top of the machine through a silver funnel.

"What does it do?" I asked.

"It creates amazing new outfits." Glissando smiled. "Whatever you put in the top of the machine gets turned into clothes. Today we're making special camouflage clothes to wear when we walk up to Bluebell Dell. The unicorns there are so shy," she added. "They run from people, but if we wear the forest fashions we're making, we'll be able to blend in with the trees and get close."

Cruella stared. "How close?"

"Oh, very close." Glissando beamed. "If we take some sparkle-berries, you may even be able to feed them."

"Awesome!" Benji said. "I've never seen a wild unicorn before."

Cruella was rummaging in her backpack now. She pulled out her journal and long black pen and pointed it at the machine. "I want to know everything about it!"

"Sure. Come and watch how it works." Glissando glided across to the machine, where the campers were still adding leaves and branches and flowers into the funnel. She peered inside. "Oh, yes, I think that's quite enough. Great job, guys. Now we just need the magic laundry detergent potion."

"Is this it?" Benji reached forward and picked up a green glass bottle on the table next to the machine. He lifted the lid and sniffed the contents.

"Ooh, it smells of Tingle Root. . . . I read this amazing book about Tingle Root. Did you know that if you put it in your shoes, it can make you invisible! Here—want to look at it, Bloom?"

But as he went to hand it to me, the bottle slipped from his grip. . . .

In the blink of an eye, Glissando swept forward and caught it before it hit the floor.

"Oops, I'm so sorry," Benji muttered, his eyes wide. "I'm a bit of a butterfingers."

"Nincompoop!" Cruella snapped. "You nearly made us all disappear!"

It wasn't a kind thing to say, but I was starting to see that Benji was a little clumsy.

"No harm done," Glissando soothed. "And you are quite correct, Benji. The potion is made with Tingle Root. Well done!"

She uncorked the green bottle and poured a dash into the funnel. "Okay—are we all ready? Good! Then you just need to press the big button on the front of the machine. Go ahead," she told one of the campers, who reached forward and pushed it.

There was a loud *KER-THUMP!*, then the machine began to shake and rattle and chug. . . . Green bubbles popped out of the funnel and a strong grassy smell filled the air. Cruella held her nose. But I liked the scent. It reminded me of sitting on the top of the lawn mower back home, Dad in his favorite hammock, using his mind to make it move.

"It's going nuts!" Benji said, as the magical laundry machine began to shudder. Then suddenly . . .

THWUMP! It stopped moving and let out a long, low whistle.

"All done," Glissando said. "Now, open the hatch."

One of the girls stepped forward and unhooked a door at the bottom of the machine. A pile of camo-colored clothes sprang out—pants, shorts, shirts, scarves. . . .

Benji picked up a camo-cap. "Wizarding wands!" he breathed. "It's the most awesome machine I've ever seen."

Glissando collected the rest of the garments and handed them around. "It looks like we've enough for everyone in this load. Slip them on over your regular clothes, then we'll go find those unicorns!"

Only Cruella didn't move. She was still staring at the magical laundry machine, tapping her long black pen against her teeth. "Can you put *anything* in that machine?" she asked Glissando.

"Oh yes. We put a bucket of apples in there yesterday and you should have seen the beautiful outfits it created—red and green and oh! They smelled so sweet."

Cruella's eyes narrowed. "So, what would

happen if you popped a cute, fluffy creature in there?" she asked. "Would it make an adorable furry hat, or some chic slippers, maybe?"

Glissando gasped. Hem's mouth dropped open. Benji's glasses steamed up. I'm sure my own eyes were boggling.

"Only joking!" Cruella laughed. "Now hand me the camo-clothes, Dahling. I *can't wait* to see the unicorns."

8

AS we walked down to Bluebell Dell, I couldn't stop thinking about what Cruella had said. *It really was a joke, right?* I told myself. *No one would actually want to put an animal in the magic laundry machine, would they?*

"Hey, I see them!" Benji, who was in front of me on the path, suddenly stopped walking and pointed off into the distance. "My glasses are on telescope mode," he explained. "And I just spotted a unicorn through the trees."

"Well done," Glissando whispered. "Now, everyone, gather round." She put her finger to her lips to make sure no one spoke, then she pulled a small golden pencil out of her sleeve and began writing in the air. A large floating bubble appeared in front of us, with instructions.

Be extra *QUIET* now, so we don't scare the unicorns away. <u>PLEASE</u> form a semi-circle and KEEP VERY STILL.

Glissando led us down the path through a thicket of tightly packed pine trees. I noticed Cruella had pushed her way to the front of the line of campers now, right behind Glissando. As we got closer to the dell, Cruella turned around and waved.

Huh . . . she actually looks excited, I thought as I waved back. *Maybe she's starting to enjoy camp after all!* Suddenly my worries about the laundry machine seemed a bit silly. *She probably just has an odd sense of humor*, I decided.

We crept through the last of the trees and

stepped out into the sunshine of a clearing full of bluebells. And that's when I saw them: a family of unicorns! For a second, I was spellbound. Even though I'd seen wild unicorns a few times before, they never failed to shock the spell-socks off me. I think it was the way their coats sparkled like gemstones in the sun, and how their silky manes hung in silver fringe around their faces. As they turned to look at us, their golden horns glistened; luckily, they didn't startle. Our camo-clothes were doing a great job of helping us to blend in.

The other campers spread out around the dell. Their eyes were wide, their mouths open. Even Cruella, who was on the other side of the circle from me, stood transfixed. And then something amazing happened. . . .

One of the smaller unicorns trotted toward me. I held my breath as it stopped to nibble the bluebells by my feet. *Could I try feeding it?* I'd never done that before. I looked across the dell at Glissando. She nodded to go ahead, so I slid my hand into the pocket of my camo jacket and pulled out a few of the sparkle-berries she'd given us earlier. Slowly, I lifted my hand toward the unicorn to offer the fruit. It sniffed the air for a moment, then reached out its neck to take the berries.

But right at that moment, there was a sudden movement from across the clearing. The unicorn turned to look. I did, too. "No! Stop!" I hissed, as Cruella lunged toward the creature, a pair of shiny scissors in her hand.

"Gotcha!" she yelled.

But the creature was faster. The unicorn

dodged Cruella's clutches and sprang away, racing after its family who had already disappeared off into the trees.

"Hey—come back!" she wailed.

The campers seemed too shocked to speak.

But I wasn't! "What are you doing?"

"What does it look like I'm doing?" She glared. "I was trying to get a lock of its tail for my journal! You could have helped me by grabbing ahold of it."

"But you can't catch a unicorn!" I said.

Glissando glided over. "Time out, team," she said soothingly. "Don't worry, Cruella, I know how hard it is to resist petting the unicorns. They're so special. Everyone is drawn to them."

"But she wasn't going to pet them," I said. "She was about to—"

"It's okay, Bloom," Glissando interrupted. "Cruella's never been around unicorns before. She doesn't know how gentle you have to be. Perhaps I can help you to learn more about them?" she

suggested, smiling at Cruella. "I have some pho-
tographs of them back at Crafty Corner. Would
you like to have one for your journal?"

Cruella shrugged.

"Come along, then, let's all return," Glissando
said. "I think it's time we had some Sparkle-Berry
Soda and a slice of Shimmer Sponge."

Hem's face lit up. "Oh, I love Shimmer Sponge."

"Then you shall help me serve it." Glissando
smiled at her. "And perhaps afterward, you'd like
to stay on for our Creative Cooking Class; we're
making color-changing cakes, today!"

"Oh yes, please," Hem said. "Baking with
magic is such fun!"

Several of the other campers looked eager to
join the cooking class, too. But Cruella's behavior
had left a bad taste in my mouth. I didn't think
even enchanted cakes would make it go away.

As we trudged through the trees, I hung back
a little, hoping to catch sight of the unicorns
again. Benji came to walk with me.

"That was so cool the way you nearly got the unicorn to take the berries from your hand," he said.

"Yeah, if only Cruella hadn't spooked them."

"That *was* a bit annoying," Benji said.

"And it's not the only strange thing she's done today. Like her comment about putting a fluffy creature in the laundry machine. And how she wanted to know everything about the Nerbit. And then there was the way she tried to squish me when you turned me into an ant—"

"An ant?" Benji cocked his head to one side.

Oops, I forgot you didn't know about that. "And you should have seen the way she reacted to Hem's dog," I said, changing the subject. "She went wild when it tried to lick her."

"I guess she doesn't like animals," Benji said.

"But that's just it," I said. "She seems to like some of them. Maybe a little *too* much . . ." I tried to imagine what Dad would say. He always told me to be fair and give people the benefit of the doubt. I sighed. "Maybe Glissando was right," I said. "If Cruella hasn't been around a lot of animals, then she probably doesn't know how to act around them.... One of my bunkmates last summer tried to shrink the unicorns so she could take them home in her trunk!"

Benji gasped. "Yikes! Do you think we should go tell someone about Cruella?"

I thought for a moment. I didn't like telling tales to grown-ups, but somehow, I couldn't completely shift the slight, squishy, worried feeling in my tummy. "Yeah," I said. "I think we should go speak to my dad. Just in case."

9

IF you ever need to find my dad, the first place to look for him is up a long ladder in the Potions Storeroom. That's where he spends most of his free time, searching through the high shelves, where he keeps his most interesting—and dangerous—spells.

"I can't believe I'm actually in here," Benji whispered as I led him through the heavy oak doors. He gazed at the thousands of bottles that lined the walls, his eyes out on stalks. "There's so much magic here!"

"Just don't touch anything," I said. "Trust me, you do not want to let some of these spells out, especially the ones with no labels. Come on, Dad's probably through the back somewhere."

The Potions Storeroom was divided into three large chambers, connected by long, narrow corridors. Each room was stuffed full of concoctions

in every sort of container, from brightly colored bottles to carved wooden boxes with jeweled lids. There were tiny clay pots and glass jars that glowed in the darkness, along with a shelf of wriggling packages tied up with brown string. There were even a few magical lamps with wispy swirls of smoke that puffed out of their spouts every so often.

As I led Benji into the second chamber, he stopped to peer at a giant purple flagon, sitting on the floor. "Oh, wow!" he said, fiddling with his lenses. "I just turned my glasses into X-ray specs, and I think that bottle has got wings inside!"

"It's probably a flying spell," I said, peering closer. "It's hard to read the label with it being so gloomy in here; Dad says too much light and heat can do funny things to potions. Come on, let's go find him. . . . Oh, and watch the steps, the last room is underground, and it gets really dark down there."

"Don't worry, my glasses will show the way." Benji tapped his frames again, and they turned neon yellow, lighting up the stone staircase in front of us. "OOH, those potions are gurgling! And what do those green ones say, Reversal Drops? Wow! They sound handy."

With a smile, I realized Benji might have been sort of a muddle-mop—that's what we call a kid at camp who is a bit of a klutz. But his enthusiasm was contagious. *And his glasses are really useful!*

The third chamber was the largest of the three storerooms and contained the oldest potions in my father's collection. Some of them hadn't been touched for hundreds of years, which explained the layers of yucky dust!

"Bloom?"

I peered through the darkness. "Oh, hi, Dad." Just as I'd expected, he was up a long ladder in the murkiest corner of the room, sorting through a row of green bottles.

"And hello to you, too, Benji." (Dad has the most amazing memory—he remembers every face and name at camp.) He climbed down from his ladder, brushing cobwebs off his long robe. "Is everything all right?"

"Er—well . . ." I never liked complaining to Dad about my bunkmates, because he always believed in giving people second chances. I remembered a time in the ice-cream parlor when I was little. The waiter accidentally dropped Dad's dessert *SPLAT* on the floor. And everyone in the café dived under the tables, expecting Dad to launch a storm of lightning bolts at them all! Dad was very embarrassed. . . . I didn't want him to think I wasn't giving Cruella a fair chance. *But this is important,* I reminded myself. *Granny Maj always tells me to follow my gut instinct. And my guts are telling me there could be a problem—even worse than when I ate that crab-apple pie I made in creative cooking class!* "It's about Cruella," I said. "She's acting a bit strange."

"In what way?" Dad said.

I glanced at Benji, but he was too busy peering at the bottles on the shelves to help me explain. "Well, she says odd things. Like at Crafty Corner, she asked what would happen if she put a fluffy creature in the magical laundry machine."

Dad chuckled. "She was probably just making a joke. Some people have an unusual sense of humor. Like your Uncle Mel."

Dad had a point. Uncle Mel was a bit of a monster. Sometimes he'd deliberately sneeze his eyeballs out! I found it freaky; Dad thought it was hilarious. "That's what I'd thought at first . . ." I said. "But it's not the only weird thing Cruella's done. We went up to Bluebell Dell and she tried to grab a unicorn to cut its tail. She said it was for her journal—"

"Some campers are quite passionate about journaling," Dad interrupted.

"Yeah, I know, but—" I stopped and thought about that for a moment. Actually, he was right. One of my recent bunkmates had caught a real live pixie and tried to press it between the pages of her journal.

"You know, Bloom, sometimes we're quick to judge people who are a little bit different," Dad said. "Look at me. Even when I changed my ways from being an evil sorcerer, no one wanted to trust me." He sighed. "Perhaps Cruella is just taking a little longer to settle into our routines. I'm sure with your help she'll begin to understand how we do things here, and—" Dad suddenly stopped talking and looked over my shoulder. "Be careful, Benji," he said. "The lid on that bottle is a little loose."

"Huh?" Benji glanced up from the potion he was holding.

Uh-oh.

"The lid—" Dad began. "Watch it doesn't—"

Too late!

The glass stopper on the bottle slipped off, smashing onto the stone floor in front of Benji. "Oops!" he muttered.

"Watch out!" Dad called, as a small object shot out of the bottle and smacked into the ceiling above us.

"Oh, my wizarding wand!" Benji gasped. "Is that a magical orb?"

"Yes," Dad said, ducking as it soared over his head and bounced off a shelf, making all the bottles wobble dangerously. "A very irritating magical orb! We must catch it before it smashes everything in the room." Dad clicked his fingers and conjured up three large butterfly nets. "Here, use these!" he said, handing one to Benji and me.

For the next few minutes, we dived around the room, chasing the orb as it ricocheted off the

walls. But orbs are sneaky. Every time one of us got close, it bounced off in a completely different direction, until—*THWACK!* It smacked into a high shelf, knocking a glass bottle off, which hit the floor and exploded!

"Achoo!" Benji sneezed so loud he dropped his net.

"Look out!" Dad called, as a thick pink liquid oozed out in front of our feet. "Quick! Both of you—run!"

10

BUT it was too late. The liquid around our feet had already begun to fizz and bubble. Then—

POP! A dozen green shoots exploded out of the puddle and shot upward before bursting open into huge roses. The strong perfume from them made my eyes water.

"It's a fast-growing flower spell," Dad said, as more shoots appeared in the puddle.

"Achoo!" Benji sneezed, and a tiny rosebud shot out of his nose. "Oh, wow, did you see that?"

"Magic always makes Benji sneeze," I explained to Dad.

Benji sneezed again, and more roses shot out of his nose. His last sneeze was so loud, it blew the orb straight into my net!

"Oh, good catch," Dad said. "And now we'd better summon up something to help with the flowers."

A flash of lightning lit up the room and a large goat appeared. It lunged toward the roses and began chomping.

"The 'Hungry Goat' spell!" Benji breathed. "That's so clever."

"Yes, and it reminds me," Dad said, glancing at an old grandfather clock in the corner of the room. "It will be your suppertime soon, so you'd better be off. Here, I'll take that, thanks—" he said, retrieving the net with the orb from me. "Oh, and Bloom," he added, as we headed for the door. "Here's something to help you with Cruella." He held out his hand, and a cabbage appeared in his palm.

"I don't understand," I said.

Dad smiled. "People are a lot like cabbages."

Benji cocked his head to one side. "You mean hard, round, and crinkly?"

"No, no, no!" Dad laughed his deep, booming, evil sorcerer sort of a cackle, and all the bottles on the shelves rattled. "I mean people have many layers, just like a cabbage. The personality they show on the outside isn't necessarily who they are on the inside. Be kind and give Cruella the chance to show you who she really is."

Benji didn't stop talking about the potions storeroom on the way back to camp. But I wasn't paying attention. I stared at the cabbage Dad had given me.

Was he right? Was I being too quick to judge Cruella? *Maybe she's one sort of person on the outside—a bit cranky with a weird sense of humor . . . though quite put together. But perhaps when you peel back the layers and get to know her, she's fun and friendly on the inside. After all, arriving at a new place with new people can be tough.*

As we reached camp, I was determined to make more of an effort with Cruella. I was just about to go find her in the bunkhouse, when the gong sounded for dinner.

"Look!" Benji said, pointing to a counselor walking past with a tray of hot dog buns. "Do you think it's a cookout tonight?"

Suddenly I realized what night it was. "Oh

yeah, it's always a barbecue on the first night of camp. Come on, the log circle is just down here."

By the time we reached the glade, most of the campers were already seated. I scanned the circle for empty spaces. "There are Hem and Cruella," I said, spotting them on the far side. Hem was chatting to our other bunkmates, while Cruella was eating an apple and writing in her journal. "Let's go sit with them—Hey, Hem! Hey, Cruella!" I called. Hem looked up and waved. But Cruella didn't hear me. She closed her journal and started watching a tiny pink squirrel that had appeared on the end of her log. "Aw, look," I whispered to Benji, "that squirrel looks like it wants a nibble of Cruella's snack."

I felt a warm glow in my belly as I saw Cruella holding the last bite of her apple out toward the little creature. *Dad's right*, I thought. *Cruella probably is kind deep down.*

But just as the squirrel got within sniffing distance of the apple—

SMACK!

Cruella slammed her journal down on its head! Or would have, if the squirrel hadn't dodged it just in time.

"Ugh!" Cruella snapped, as the squirrel zipped away, racing up the first tree it could find.

I was frozen to the spot. *Had I really just seen her try to squish a squirrel?*

"Oh, hello, Zoom," she said, suddenly noticing me. "Did you see how that creature tried to bite me! If I hadn't had my journal to defend myself, it might have taken my fingers off!" She shuddered.

Come on, Bloom! Give Cruella a chance, I reminded myself. *Perhaps she really did think the* squirrel was going to bite her. *After all, she doesn't know that the animals here are friendly.*

"So, have you come to fetch my supper?" Cruella added. "Good! Because I'm famished."

I glanced at the cabbage in my hand, then back at Cruella. *Maybe I just need to peel back some more layers.*

11

"**NO**, no, you can't take a unicorn home in your trunk— Huh?" I woke up with a start, my heart beating fast and that strange, squishy feeling back in my belly. *Calm down, Bloom*, I told myself. *It was just a nightmare*. I picked up the little clock on my nightstand. Half past midnight.

I'd hung out with Cruella all evening, throughout dinner and the campfire sing-along that followed. She'd mostly ignored me, writing in her journal and gazing off into the distance. Even at bedtime, she hadn't said much, apart from telling us all that we'd better not snore or she'd put clothes pegs on our noses. I'd fallen into a restless sleep.

Now I glanced around at the dozing lumps around the room. Hem and our other bunkmates were fast asleep—and so was Cruella. *See, it was just a silly nightmare*, I told myself. *No one is out catching unicorns!* I lay back on my pillow and closed my eyes, and I was just drifting off again when I heard it. A soft tap-tapping noise on the window by my bunk.

"Bloom!" I heard a voice call from outside. "Are you there?"

"Benji?" I climbed out of bed and lifted the curtain to peer out. I blinked at the light from my friend's glasses glowing brightly in the darkness. "What is it?" I whispered.

"I need your help," he said. "I'm worried about the Nerbit."

I crept softly over to the door so I didn't wake anyone, and slipped outside.

Benji's face was lit up by the moon. "Look," he said, holding up Cruella's journal. "One of the counselors found this by the campfire. I said I'd give it back to her tomorrow. Only, when I was getting ready for bed, I accidentally dropped it. . . ."

I smiled. That sounded like something Benji would do.

"And it fell open at this page," he added, showing me a sheet of drawings.

I looked closer and tried to make sense of what I was seeing. "Shocking spells!" I gasped, a sudden shiver passing through me. "She's drawn the Nerbit as a hat!" I pushed the hair out of my eyes and looked again. "B-b-but she wouldn't *actually* do that. They're just doodles."

"What if they're not just doodles?" Benji said. "What if they're plans?" He gave a sniff. "I

*must dye color

SO FLUFFY!

more glam?
accessories?

told her the secret code for the Big Barn, so she could easily take the Nerbit. And it would be all my fault."

"But she's in bed, see...." I opened the door just a crack so he could peek inside.

Benji tapped his glasses a couple of times and looked again. "That's not Cruella," he whispered. "That's pillows! I can see them with my X-ray glasses."

"What? It can't be." I tiptoed back into the room, across to Cruella's bunk, my heart pounding in my chest. If Benji was wrong, she was not going to be happy about being woken up. I took a deep breath and gently peeled back the covers....

"Walloping wishing wells!" I looked again at the pillows arranged to look like a person. *Surely, she hasn't really gone to take the Nerbit?!* It was too horrible to believe. And yet . . . what other explanation could there be? After everything I'd said about giving Cruella the benefit of the doubt. And now . . . I squeezed my hands into tight fists. It was time to step in—for the good of the camp. *She's not going to get away with this!*

I darted back to the door, being careful not to wake any of my other bunkmates.

"Give me two minutes," I whispered to Benji. "Don't worry—we'll save the Nerbit!"

12

A few moments later, I reappeared, my back-pack filled with useful things I thought we might need, including a flashlight and my *in-case-of-emergencies* wand.

"Come on," I whispered to Benji. "We'll take the shortcut."

We crept quietly past the cabins—careful not to disturb anyone—then climbed over a fence and set off down the track toward the Big Barn. We were halfway there, when I spotted something twinkling up ahead. I peered into the gloom. . . .

"Uh-oh!" I muttered, grabbing Benji's sleeve. "That looks like a Glow-Cart. One of the counselors is heading our way."

Before Benji could reply, the cart suddenly increased its speed, zooming straight for us.

"Watch out!" I cried, waggling my hands in the air to make sure the driver could see us. "Stop!"

We just had time to throw ourselves into the bushes, as the Glow-Cart roared up the track. But as it drew level with us, its wheels skidded on a patch of mud and it veered into a strip of long grass and stalled.

"Curses!" the driver muttered.

I shone my flashlight to see who it was, but their face was hidden by a red dotty scarf tied under their chin. "Hello?" I called. "Are you okay?" The driver turned to look at me, blinking under the glare of my beam. "Crashing cauldrons!" I spluttered. "It's Cruella!"

"Hello, Dahlings!" she said, a nasty smirk on her face. "A bit late for a walk, isn't it?"

"What are you doing?" I cried. "Campers aren't allowed in the Glow-Carts."

"I told you, I'm an excellent driver!" Cruella gripped the steering wheel more tightly. "Though my Rolls is far smoother than this rust bucket!" She revved the engine and it stalled again.

Benji nudged me and pointed to a box by her side. "It's the Nerbit!" he whispered. "I can see it through the case with my X-ray glasses."

Cruella grinned, showing sharp little pointy teeth. "Oh yes . . . I've just been up to the Big Barn to collect my fluffy little passenger." She gave a shrill laugh. The type of laugh that could have shattered windows. Then she revved the cart's engine once more and reversed out of the grass. "So long, nincompoops!" she yelled, as she shot off down the track, leaving a cloud of fairy dust behind her.

For a moment, we just stood there, our mouths open, our eyes blinking. Then—

"Quick!" Benji gasped, tugging on my sleeve. "We've got to stop her! She must be heading for Crafty Corner."

"But there's no way we can catch up. We'll have to go find my dad."

"No!" Benji looked close to tears. "If we tell your dad, he'll find out it was me who gave her the code to the Big Barn, and he won't let me help with the animals again. Can't we stop her ourselves?"

I thought about it for a moment. I definitely

didn't want to get Benji in trouble. And even if we did go to find my dad, I wasn't exactly sure where to look for him. Dad never slept much, which meant he could be anywhere—repairing fences or fixing buildings in the dark, talking to the creatures of the night. By the time we found him, it might be too late. . . .

"Please, Bloom!" Benji's face was pale, his eyes pleading.

"Okay. But there's no way we can catch up with Cruella, unless . . ." I swallowed. *Unless we break some big rules*. But then hadn't Dad told us all in class that it was important to take risks? "I guess we'll need to borrow a Glow-Cart, too," I said. "Come on, there's a garage by the welcome booth just behind the cabins."

Benji's face lit up. "Really? You'd do that for me? Oh, Bloom, you're the best! And don't worry, I know everything about Glow-Carts. After I read about them in the brochure, I borrowed a book from the library and learned how to start them and—"

"Um—that's great," I interrupted. "But we'd better get a move on."

As we climbed back over the fence, I paused and looked out at the Enchanted Woods below. "We'll need to be extra careful," I whispered. "The forest can be a bit spooky at night."

"Really?" Benji's eyes boggled.

"Yeah, but don't worry," I said. "If we stick together, we should be fine."

Though I tried to sound confident, I was starting to feel a little wobbly. The Enchanted Woods were fun during the day, but at night, when the friendly trees went to sleep and the flowers weren't singing . . . I shuddered. Anything could happen!

13

"OOPS, sorry!"

It was Benji's third attempt at starting the Glow-Cart, and so far, all he'd managed to do was make it judder, shake, and bunny-hop toward the garage door.

"Don't worry," I said. "Take your time." But inside I was quaking. I tried not to think about what might be happening to the Nerbit. Not to mention the small issue of us breaking one of the camp's strictest rules.

"I'm sure the book said you just press this button and turn the dial to 'glow.'"

"Maybe it's low on fairy dust?" I suggested.

But just at that moment the engine rumbled into life, and the cart began to sparkle.

"Oh, wow! We're moving!" Benji pressed the accelerator pedal down as far as it would go, and we shot out of the garage. "Watch out, Cruella!" he called.

"Whoa! Not so fast!" I cried, dangerously close to bouncing out of the cart.

"Don't worry," Benji said. "I think I've got the hang of— Ahh!"

We hit a bump in the path and took off into the air before landing back down with a *THUMP!*

"Ugh!" I gritted my teeth as we nearly veered off the path into a tree. *Uh-oh! It looks like Benji's just as much of a muddle-mop behind the wheel!* "Hey—maybe I should drive?"

But Benji couldn't hear me. We were whizzing down the path now, passing through the entrance to the woods. I felt my heart begin to thud again. *Be brave, Bloom!* But it was hard. The sleeping tree branches above us blocked out all the moonlight. And everywhere around us were strange noises. Rustlings. Whisperings. Twigs cracking under our wheels! "Whoa!" I muttered, as the cart bounced over a tree root and a shadow shot out of the undergrowth in front of us. I shone my flashlight to see what it was, but the creature had hidden itself again.

"Maybe the cart's lights are attracting the beasties," Benji whispered. "I'll change my glasses into night-vision goggles so I can see them lurking."

"Genius!" *Benji might be a bit of a muddle-mop,*

I thought, *but he's also quite smart.* "Let's switch. Tell me when you see something," I said. "And I'll take us in a different direction."

The plan worked. We managed to avoid most of the bothersome beasties skulking in the dark— even a pesky pack of Swamp Pugs who snuffled past us while we zoomed up another path. But halfway to Crafty Corner, our luck changed.

The cart began to slow. Its lights were shining less brightly now. Then it coughed. And hiccupped. And stopped altogether.

"Maybe it ran out of fairy dust?" I suggested.

Benji groaned. "But what about the Nerbit?"

"Don't worry, it's not much farther," I said, clambering out of the cart. "We can run the rest of the way."

Just then I felt a tickle on my arm. *Huh?* I spun around and heard a snigger from somewhere in the darkness. "Um—I think we should get moving," I whispered to Benji. "We've got company— Hey!" I turned quickly and this time

I saw it. A tiny figure diving into the bushes. *Tickle Tots!* I groaned. They were the annoying preschool pixies who liked to play tricks on humans—and at the top of their fun list: tickling!

"Eek!" Benji jumped. "Did you just tickle my neck, Bloom?"

"It's the Tickle Tots."

"The who?"

I didn't need to explain because there was a whistle from the bushes, and suddenly they all appeared at once. A dozen preschool pixies, swarming around our ankles, tickling us with their glowing feather sticks.

"Ooh! Hee-hee!" Benji giggled, trying to dodge out of their reach. But the more he squealed the more pixies appeared.

"Hey! Stop that!" I said, as one poked her feather stick almost up my nose. I dropped my backpack and tried to swipe the tickle sticks away. "Benji!" I puffed. "We need to make a run for it."

"Argh! Ha-hee-hee," Benji mumbled, wriggling as the young pixies attacked his legs with their feathers. "It's like being covered in itchy ants!"

"Shush!" I whispered. "You really don't want to attract their parents. They don't just tickle. They pinch!"

"Hoi!" I cried, as one of the pixies grabbed my flashlight. "Give that back!" I tried to take it. But the pixie dived away, waggling the flashlight in the air like a trophy. *Grrrr!* I'd had enough now. There was only one thing to do. . . .

I grabbed my emergency wand out of my backpack and tried to remember the spell I'd seen Glissando and the other counselors do on treat night.

"Um—*sugar sugar* . . . er, *nice and sweet* . . ." I said, waggling my wand in the air. ". . . *Conjure up a tasty treat!*"

"Achoo!" the smell of magic in the air instantly made Benji sneeze again. It was so loud, he blew three Tickle Tots off their feet.

But they were all too busy gazing at the glowing pink clouds that had appeared above their heads, now drifting gently down toward them.

"Mmmm, cotton candy!" one of the Tickle Tots squeaked as a piece landed in its open mouth.

Suddenly they were all grabbing and gobbling the sweet cloud into their mouths. I picked up my backpack and clutched Benji's arm. "Run!"

We dashed away, heads down, arms pumping, racing along the path. We passed lots of weird-looking creatures: were-weasels, monster mice, even a flying skunk that whizzed over our heads in a large, whiffy cloud of stink!

"Hey, what's that over there?" Benji panted, as we leaned against a tree to catch our breath. "It looks like a Glow-Cart. . . ."

We crept over to take a look. The cart's engine was silent, the twinkling lights fading.

Benji turned to look at me, his glasses glowing in the dark. "Do you think it was the cart Cruella was driving?"

I nodded. "I guess it ran out of fairy dust, too, but look—" I reached out my hand toward it. "The cart's still warm, which means she can't be that far ahead."

"Especially if she's carrying the Nerbit's box," Benji added.

"Yep, and don't forget Cruella only wears high heels. That should slow her down!"

Benji's shoulders seemed to relax a little, and he smiled.

"Let's go!" I felt a surge of hope in my tummy as we set off, scanning the woods for any sign of her. Cruella was not going to get away with this, not if I could help it!

14

BUT we didn't catch up with Cruella. And soon we saw the lights of Crafty Corner shining brightly in the distance.

"Oh no!" Benji panted. "I hope we're not too late."

"Me too," I said, my heart beating faster. I reckoned Cruella must have found another way to get to Crafty Corner—a magical broomstick, perhaps, or some springy spell-socks so she could bounce her way over. Or maybe she'd trapped a flying deer and flown across the wood.

We raced up the path and along the front of the cabin to the windows.

"There she is!" Benji gasped. Cruella stood in the middle of the room drawing pictures on a large blackboard. They looked a lot like the hat sketches Benji had shown me in her journal, though much more detailed. I shivered.

"There's the Nerbit!" Benji pointed to the creature carrier box on the table next to the blackboard. The Nerbit's trunk could just be seen poking out through the bars.

Cruella suddenly threw the chalk down and stalked over to the table and pulled the Nerbit out. "Come along now," I heard her say. "No fussing!" She carried the wriggling Nerbit to the laundry machine. Then she clambered up onto the stool next to it and began trying to squish the creature into the silver funnel.

"No!" I banged on the window. "Stop!"

Cruella spun around. The shock on her face disappeared when she saw it was us. She stuck out her tongue, then went back to trying to squash the Nerbit into the machine.

"Quick!" I cried. "We've got to get inside!"

Benji was already running for the door. "It's bolted!" he groaned.

"Try the unlocking spell," I suggested. "The one from the Big Barn. Cruella!" I shouted again, banging even louder on the window. "Let the Nerbit go!"

She paid no attention. "Get in, you beast!" she cried, pressing the wriggling Nerbit into the funnel.

But the creature was putting up a fight. It spread its paws out like a starfish.

"It's no good!" Benji called to me. "The unlocking spell doesn't work. I think she's barricaded the door on the other side."

"Go around the back," I said. "There's another door. I'll keep distracting her." I thumped on the window again. "Cruella! You're going to be in so much trouble. . . ."

She turned and glared at me, then hopped off the stool with the Nerbit still writhing in her arms. After shoving the creature back into its carrier, she came to the window, her face red. "Leave NOW!" she yelled at me. "You're spoiling everything."

Keep her talking, I told myself. *Give Benji time to find another way in.* "Um—hey—that was a clever idea with the pillows in your bed."

Her face relaxed a little. "Ha!" she snorted. "It's the oldest trick in the book! Though I find it always works best with the most luxurious, mulberry silk pillows. Now go away. I'm busy!"

"Wait—" I said desperately. "Um—how did you get here so quickly? We found your Glow-Cart conked out in the woods. I guess you must have been running really fast. . . ."

She rolled her eyes. "I despise running. I took the magic speed tunnel."

"The what?" I blinked at her.

"Don't you remember your little friend talking about them? He said they were one of the camp's mysterious secrets. Well, I found one when that tiresome Glow-Cart broke down!"

Huh? "You mean the tunnels really do exist?"

"I thought YOU were the expert here." Cruella smirked at me. "There's an entrance right where you're standing now."

I glanced down and tried to see what she was describing.

"Behind the giggle-berry bush. Shame you didn't know about it before—you might have got here in time to save the little Nerbit!" She snorted. "But it's too late now." And with that, she reached up and pulled down a window blind, blotting out my view.

15

"**BENJI!**" I yelled, as I ran around the side of the craft center. "Did you open the back door?"

"No. It's locked, too." Benji was on his hands and knees, using his glasses to light up a woodpile, which he was rummaging through. "But don't worry. I've got an idea. There's a loose window in the bathroom. I just need to find the right stick, and I think I'll be able to open it—oh, this one looks good." He held up a sturdy twig, then led me over to one of the windows and pointed out a small gap between the window and the frame. "Now I just need to push the stick in, like this. . . ." He pushed down hard, and the window groaned. "My mom had to do this once," he explained, as he continued to press down on the twig, "when she lost her door keys. She's a bit of a muddle-mop!"

I smiled.

Just then, there was a loud *CRACK!* And the window popped open.

"Great work, Benji!" I clambered over the sill and dropped down onto the floor.

Benji followed, and we crept toward the bathroom door that led into the main part of the craft center.

"Ready?" I mouthed.

He nodded.

I took a deep breath, then threw open the door.

"Stop right there!" I yelled at Cruella, who was back on the stool by the magical laundry machine. "Hey—where's the Nerbit?" I looked around the room, but the carrier was empty and there was no sign of the little creature anywhere.

Cruella gave a smug smile. "In the machine, of course. It turns out, the best way to squish a creature into a small place is to tickle it. And now I just need to add the laundry detergent potion," she said, reaching for the green bottle.

"No!" I lunged forward to stop her, but Benji tugged me back.

"Watch it!" he said. "Thumbtacks!" He pointed to the floor around the laundry machine, which was covered in spiky pins.

"Ha!" Cruella cackled. "Do you like my booby trap?"

I gritted my teeth. "Quick! We need a broom to brush them up," I told Benji. "Check the cupboard in the bathroom."

But Cruella had nearly finished adding the laundry detergent potion. "Why are you doing this?" I shouted.

She looked up, then shrugged. "Why shouldn't I? I want a hat. A special hat. A hat that only I will own. No one else has ever had a hat made of Nerbit fluff! I will be special."

"But why does that matter?"

She snorted. "Because I deserve nice, perfect, shiny things! And with a Nerbit hat—a hat made from one of the rarest creatures in the world, I will look *amazing*!" Her eyes sparkled. "And I won't stop there!" She pointed to the wall display behind her, which was covered in campers'

artwork. "Perhaps I'll make something else, to go with my hat. Some penguin-skin boots, maybe. Or a parrot-feather sweater. Or how about a pair of panda-fur pants! What do you think? Which one would make the best outfit?"

I glanced at the pictures behind her, at the doodles of fluffy kittens and brightly colored birds and cute dotty-coated puppies.... "But don't you care about animals?" I said.

She cocked her head to one side as though she was actually considering my question.

Then— "Umm, no. Animals are *messy* and unpredictable," she said. "Now go away!" And she went back to adding the laundry detergent.

I looked around for something to stop her with—a ball, a bucket of water—or a spell! *Of course! My emergency wand!* I reached into my backpack, and as soon as my fingers wrapped around it, I had a flashback to the spell we'd done in Creature Care Class. Dad's words came back to me: *You can't understand an animal until you've been one yourself. . . . Maybe if Cruella becomes an animal,* I thought, *then she'll treat them better.*

Cruella was already reaching for the big button on the front of the machine as I lifted my wand high into the air. I glanced at the pictures on the wall as I began to say the words. . . . *Broomsticks crossed, I remember them in the right order.*

"*Dibble, Dabble, Fur and Claw,*" I said, swishing a figure eight toward Cruella's head. "*Transform this person, tail to paw.*"

"Found one!" Benji called, returning with a broom. "Achoo!"

A Benji sneeze! The spell must be working!

Cruella looked at me in horror, her hand still hovering in front of the machine. Then abruptly she fell off the stool, dropping onto all fours. She began stretching and moving and changing and wriggling and—woofing! And suddenly she was a dog.

"A dalmatian!" Benji grinned. "Awesome transformation!"

"That one looked so fun and friendly," I said, pointing to the doodle of a dotty, spotty puppy on the wall.

Cruella let out a long, cheerful bark, then bounded over to us. Benji just managed to sweep a path through the carpet of thumbtacks as she threw herself at us, wagging her tail and licking my hand. "Oh, hi!" I said, chuckling and tickling her ears. "You're a lovely dog, aren't you! Hey, Benji, maybe Dad was right. There *was* a nicer person hidden under all of Cruella's cabbage layers. . . . Her dog self is WAY kinder than the human one."

16

A moment later, we rescued the Nerbit. Benji turned one of his lenses into a screwdriver, and we were able to take off the back of the magical laundry machine. The Nerbit's fluff was a bit squished, but after brushing off the laundry detergent and giving it a handful of giggle-berries from the bush outside, the Nerbit seemed in better spirits. We put it back in its creature carrier, and it nodded off right away.

"Probably exhausted," Benji said as we left the craft center.

"I'm not sure what Dad will say about the broken window," I said, pulling the door behind us.

But Benji was staring at the sky. "Oh no," he groaned. "I think it'll be light soon. I was hoping we could return the Nerbit to the Big Barn before anyone noticed it was missing."

"Don't worry. I may know a shortcut." I peered behind the giggle-berry bush. And then I saw it. "There! A trapdoor ... According to Cruella it leads to the secret tunnel network that you told us about."

"What?" Benji gasped. "No way!"

I lifted the trapdoor and peered down inside. "It's so dark down there."

"Let me shine my glasses inside."

Even with the light from Benji's lenses, we still couldn't see much. But then—

"Look!" he said, pointing to a tiny sign on the inside of the tunnel. "It's got instructions written on it. '**Welcome to this tunnel station,**'" he read. "'**Just say the name of your destination.**' Ooh!"

I hesitated. *Has this been properly tested? Will it be safe to use?* Then I saw the hope on Benji's face. "I guess we'll just need to trust it works," I said. "Have you got the Nerbit? Oh, and what about Cruella?"

For the last few minutes, Cruella the dalmatian had been zooming around the woods, ears flapping, tail wagging, finding sticks and sniffing out smells. At that moment she came bounding toward us, dragging an enormous tree branch behind her.

"Um—how are we going to get her into the tunnel?" Benji whispered.

"Hmmmm . . . My dog Muffins will go anywhere if you throw a ball. Perhaps if we toss one down the tunnel, she'll follow it."

"Do we have a ball?" Benji asked.

I was about to say no, when suddenly I remembered the cabbage. I pulled it out of my backpack. "It looks like a ball, right?"

Benji grinned. "Perfect!"

"Here, Cruella!" I called, patting my leg to get her attention. I threw the cabbage in the air. She dropped the tree branch, gave a loud bark, and then bounded over, her tail wagging.

"Chase the ball, now, girl," I said. "Go on! Fetch!" I threw the cabbage into the hole, and she dived after it. I just had time to say "Big Barn" before she vanished into the darkness.

"Well, she's gone somewhere," Benji said, peering down into the tunnel.

I picked up the Nerbit's carrier. "I guess it's our turn." I crouched down and dangled my legs into the abyss with the Nerbit's box on my lap. I shivered. It felt cold down there. *I hope it's not stuffed with spiders and full of dust! Broomsticks crossed!* Then I pushed myself off. "Big Barn!" I yelled as the tunnel sucked me down. Suddenly I was whizzing through the darkness, clutching the Nerbit's carrier to my chest. It was a bit like being in a slide at the swimming pool. Only I couldn't see anything! *What if someone's coming the other way?* I suddenly thought, expecting at any moment to smash into another tunnel traveler. But just then—*POP!* The tunnel spat me out on the grass in front of the Big Barn.

"Whoa! That was so fast. Are you okay, little guy?" I peered into the Nerbit's box; somehow it was still asleep. Just then I remembered Benji was only a few seconds behind me—

POP! He burst out onto the grass, and I only just managed to scramble out of his way.

"Thundering thunderbolts!" Benji panted. "That was—um—er—" But he seemed to have left most of his words behind in the tunnel. "Out of this world!" he finally managed to splutter.

"Definitely unforgettable," I said, flipping shut the trapdoor. I wobbled on my feet as I tried to stand. "I think I left my stomach at the other end."

"Can we do it again?" Benji asked.

"Um—you'd better go put the Nerbit back," I said, "while I try and find Cruella."

While Benji returned the Nerbit to the Big Barn, I looked around for the dalmatian. But all I could find was the cabbage, smooshed on a patch of long grass. "Cruella!" I called, trying not to shout too loud in case I woke anyone. "Where are you?"

And then suddenly she charged out of the trees, ears flapping, tail wagging, a stinky old boot in her mouth.

Benji reappeared and laughed as Cruella tossed the boot in the air. "She's so funny! Can we leave her as a dog?"

It was tempting. Cruella was so much better behaved as a pup. *But what would Dad say? And wouldn't Cruella's family miss her?* "Nah, I think we need to turn her back—only—" A sudden worry hit me. "I'm not sure how. Dad didn't teach us the reversal spell, did he?"

"Ooh, ooh, I know!" Benji's glasses fogged up with excitement. "The jar of Reversal Drops in the Potions Storeroom. Couldn't we go fetch them?"

I swallowed hard, remembering the chaos earlier, when Benji had been let loose in Dad's Potions Storeroom. And this time, Dad wouldn't be there to sort out the mess. "Um—I don't know— Oh, hey—where's Cruella going?"

She bounded toward the trees, barking loudly.

"What's she spotted?" I said, squinting into the distance to see. But then— "Oh no! Phoenix chicks! Stop, Cruella! You can't chase them; they haven't learned to fly yet!"

Benji and I dashed over, but luckily the chicks had already managed to squidge themselves inside a hole in the tree to hide. Cruella was howling and scratching at the bark.

"No, Cruella!" I said, pulling her away. "Leave

them alone." Even as a dog she was a danger to other creatures. "We'd better go find those Reversal Drops," I said. "And quickly."

She dodged away from me, and dived after a golden squirrel that was scampering past. "Stop!" I yelled, but it was too late. In seconds she'd disappeared into the trees. *Urgh! We need another cabbage. Or a dog whistle. Dad always uses one with Muffins.*

"Should we chase after her?" Benji asked.

I scanned the woods trying to catch sight of her, then shook my head.

"She'll just keep chasing animals until we change her back. Come on, let's go get the drops first."

17

SNEAKING into Dad's Potions Storeroom unsupervised was probably the scariest thing I'd ever done. Ever since I was small, Dad had warned me about the dangers of touching magical concoctions without a grown-up close by. He liked to tell the story about how he'd played with one of his great-grandma's vanishing potions when he was a boy, and one of his fingers had disappeared. It never came back!

I opened the heavy oak doors with shaking hands and my heart banging in my chest. If anything happened in here—if we accidentally broke a bottle or dropped a pot, we'd be in big trouble.

"Oh, wow! I'd forgotten how awesome this place is," Benji said, using his glasses to light up the first chamber. He leaned in to take a closer look at a shelf of bottles and nearly tripped over a wooden box.

"Careful!" I gasped. I bit my lip and resisted the urge to ask Benji to wait outside. I needed his help; with no flashlight, Benji's glasses were the only light we had.

"Ooh, look at this!" Benji breathed, peering at a small tub. "The label says 'swim like a fish.' I'd love to try that."

"No! Stop!" I said, as he reached to pick it up. "We mustn't touch anything, remember."

"Oops, sorry, I forgot."

"Come on. You said you saw the drops in the second chamber, right?"

As we crept along the dark corridor to the next room, I wondered what Dad would say if he saw us.

"I was just thinking," Benji said. "It's a good thing we left Cruella outside. Her waggy tail could have done a lot of damage in here."

I laughed nervously.

We entered the second chamber, and Benji scanned the room. "I'm sure they were around here." He pointed to a shelf that was groaning with heavy jars. (It really was groaning; I think some of the shelves in the storeroom may actually be alive!)

I looked closer. "Maybe Dad moved the drops ... he does that, a lot."

"Wait—no! I think they might be ..." Benji leaned in to look more closely, then lost his balance and fell forward, bumping into the shelves and making the potions rattle wildly.

I glanced up. One of the smallest jars on the highest shelf wobbled. *Oh no!* It started plummeting toward his head.

"Benji!" I yelled. "Watch out!"

Just at the right moment, Benji somehow managed to step back, look up, and—

"Blundering broomsticks!" he spluttered, as he caught the jar in his arms. "How did that happen?"

Before I could reply—

"Bloom!" he squealed, pointing to the label on the jar. "You're never going to believe this. . . . It's the Reversal Drops!"

He handed it to me and I gazed at the jar of shiny green drops. "How on earth . . ."

He grinned at me. "Must be magic!" I chuckled. Somehow Benji's muddle-mopness had led us to the exact potion we needed.

"So how many drops do we need?" Benji asked.

I read the instructions on the label:

"To reverse a spell, you must eat,

Five whole drops, nice and neat!"

I unscrewed the lid. "If you hold out your hand, I'll count them out."

After he'd put the drops in my backpack, I replaced the lid on the jar and carefully put it back onto a shelf. It wasn't the right shelf. *But maybe Dad won't notice. Broomsticks crossed!*

I breathed a sigh of relief as we returned to the first chamber. The front doors were still open, and thin shafts of early morning sunshine were beginning to shine through. Now all we had to do was find Cruella!

But just as I went to step outside—

"What are these?" Benji asked, hanging back a little.

I peered at the large stack of purple eggs he was pointing to. "They're mystery eggs," I said. "Each one contains a different spell."

Benji's eyes sparkled.

"But they're not always good ones," I said quickly. "Sometimes, they can contain a snow-storm. Or a bad smell. Or even an annoying tune. I once had an egg that contained a tiny tornado. You should have seen the mess it made."

"I wonder what's in this one?" Benji picked up the egg on the top of the pile. "I'll check with my X-ray specs!"

"No! They're very fragile."

Too late. The egg slipped from his fingers and smashed onto the stone floor. "Achoo!" Benji looked down at the shattered shell. His glasses and face turned the same bright red. "I'm so sorry."

I sighed. From muddle-mopped brilliance to klutzy catastrophe in about two minutes.

Luckily there wasn't a tornado inside. A tiny orange cloud was now drifting up from the floor. It floated above our heads and then—

Peep! Peep! Peep!

"Oh no," I groaned, putting my hands over my ears. "Whistling clouds are the worst! Quick! Let's slip outside. We might be able to leave it in here."

We tried to sneak away, closing the door behind us. But the noisy cloud squeezed itself through a tiny gap under the door.

Peep! Peep! Peep!

"How can we stop it?!" Benji cried over the shrill trilling above his head.

"It'll probably wear off soon!" I said. "Broomsticks crossed!"

Meanwhile we still had to find Cruella. I glanced across toward the woods. "I still don't see the dalmatian. . . ."

"Huh?" Benji cocked his head. "I CAN'T HEAR YOU!"

I frowned. *I can't even hear me!* I tried to waft the noisy cloud away, but it just seemed to make it mad.

PEEP! PEEP! PEEP!

"Come on," I said, beckoning to Benji to follow. "WE NEED TO FIND CRUELLA!"

"WHAT DID YOU SAY?" Benji shouted back.

Urgh! I closed my eyes and clamped my hands

over my ears. *How are we going to find Cruella when I can't even think straight?*

But just then I heard a new sound.

RUFF, RUFF?

I opened my eyes. "Cruella?"

And there she was. Tail wagging. Ears flapping. Tongue dangling out of her mouth. She charged across the grass toward us. *Wow, I guess the cloud* does *sound like a dog whistle.*

I looked at Benji, who gave me a thumbs-up.

CRUELLA was so pleased to see us that I managed to pop the Reversal Drops into her mouth while she licked our hands.

But nothing happened.

"Maybe it takes the drops a little while to work," I said, as we walked back toward the bunks. The whistling cloud had drifted off now. Meanwhile, Cruella was running around our feet. She'd found a large muddy stick and was proudly carrying it in her mouth.

As we reached our bunk, I yawned. My eyelids suddenly felt like someone had tied giant cauldrons to them. "What time is it?" I asked.

Benji touched his glasses. "Just after five, according to my lens clock."

"Less than two hours until breakfast." I yawned again. "I'm exhausted. Time for bed.

Hopefully, Cruella will have transformed back by the time we get up again. Come on, girl," I called to her. "Hey—you can't take that stick into the bunk with you; you'll get your sheets all dirty!" But Cruella refused to drop it. And I was too tired to argue. "Night, Benji," I called softly as Cruella and I slipped into our bunk.

"Night, Bloom," Benji replied.

But I didn't hear him. I was already curled up in my bed, my eyes closing, drifting off into a deep, deep sleep.

After what seemed like about two seconds, I felt a hard poke on my arm.

"Hoi! Wake up!"

Huh? I opened my eyes to find Cruella's cranky face looming over me. "Oh, phew! You're back to normal!" I smiled at her. "The Reversal Drops worked."

"What?" Cruella scowled down at me. "I don't know what you're talking about. But look at this! I found it in my bed." She dangled the muddy stick in front of me. "Did you let that rotten girl's dog back in here last night?"

I sat up, blinking in the bright sunlight now pouring through the bunkhouse window.

"And that's not all," Cruella went on. "I found dirty paw prints all over my blankets. And the smell . . ." She shuddered. "The whole bunk stinks of dog! And I had such a terrible nightmare last night. I dreamed I WAS a dog."

I tried not to laugh.

"Get up and help me pack!" Cruella said. "I'm not staying here a moment longer."

I looked around the bunk. Cruella's possessions were laid out in neat piles on the floor, with her open trunk next to them. "Um—where is everyone?" I asked, suddenly noticing our bunkmates weren't there.

"Breakfast!" Cruella growled. "Not every person is as lazy as you, Plume!"

I clambered out of bed.

"My limo is collecting me in ten minutes," Cruella said, tossing me the sheets off her bed. "Fold these and pack them in my trunk and be quick about it."

As I started to help, I thought about how, on paper, Cruella wasn't the worst kid to live with—neat, tidy, and generally clean (apart from her time as a dog). Then I shivered, thinking of the poor Nerbit and how close it had been to becoming a fur hat! *Nope. Polished and organized doesn't necessarily make the best bunkmate!*

"Stop dithering!" Cruella yelled. "Get a move on!"

Definitely best she goes home, I decided, as I began to pack faster.

✦

Within ten minutes, Cruella's chauffeur had arrived, and she'd left camp forever. I couldn't say I was sorry.

"Hey, Bloom! Over here." Benji waved as I headed into the breakfast hall. I picked up a plate of waffles and went to join him—wiping away some of the crumbs he'd dropped on the table before I sat down.

"So, I just saw Cruella leave," Benji said, his eyes wide, his mouth full of waffle.

"Yeah, I guess it's a shame it didn't work out," I said, using my napkin to mop up some orange juice Benji had sloshed out of his glass.

"Yeah, but the camp creatures will be a whole lot safer without her," Benji said, adding another squirt of syrup to his waffles, and spilling a large dollop onto the table in the process. "And there's more good news. . . ."

I looked up from my plate. "There is?"

Benji's eyes sparkled. "I've learned a new spell for making whipped cream! My bunkmate showed me. Want some for your waffles?"

"Um—"

But Benji had already pulled a pencil out of his pocket. "It works just as well as a wand," he explained, as he lifted the pencil above my plate.

"*Yummy, scrummy, milky daydream . . . Make me a jug of freshly whipped cream! —Achoo!*"

As he sneezed there was a loud *BANG!* And a bucketful of whipped cream appeared above us and splattered its contents across the table. It covered us, the floor, and the two kids at the next table!

"Benji!" I wailed, wiping the cream out of my eyes.

Then I looked at his face covered in runny cream, and I couldn't help myself—I burst out laughing. Benji might not be the neatest kid in camp, but he was the most enthusiastic one I'd ever met. Plus, without his clumsiness, Cruella would still be a dog wandering the forest!

"I am so sorry about all the mess," Benji said.

"But on the bright side, I was thinking ... now that Cruella's gone home, you might get a cool new bunkmate."

I froze. *A new bunkmate?* I hadn't thought of that.

"Ah, there you are, Bloom!" I turned to see Dad standing behind me. He does that a lot—just appears from nowhere. "And good morning to you, too, Benji. I've just heard that Cruella has decided to go home early...."

I looked at Benji. His eyes were wide. My throat suddenly felt a little dry.

"I just wanted to thank you both," Dad said, "for trying so hard to help Cruella settle in."

What? No mention of Glow-Carts and secret tunnels?

"Um—no problem," Benji muttered.

"Er—yeah, it's a pity she couldn't stay longer," I mumbled.

Dad nodded. "No matter. Perhaps she'll come back next year." He turned to go, then stopped.

"By the way, Bloom . . . Did you find the cabbage useful?"

I thought about it for a moment. When I'd first met Cruella, I'd liked how neat and tidy she was and actually thought I'd found the sort of bunkmate I'd been dreaming about. And even when she was being mean, I hoped that underneath her cranky layers, I'd find a better person. *But I didn't.* I was just about to tell Dad that his cabbage idea didn't work, when I looked across at Benji, who was now trying to flip the cream off the table with the menu.

Wait! The cabbage idea doesn't work for Cruella, but it does for Benji! He might be a total muddle-mop on the outside. . . . I ducked as a lump of cream flew over my head and landed on one of the kids at the table next to us. *But underneath he is so much more. He's got layers of bravery and kindness and creativity and he knows so much about magic! Plus, he's shown me that a little messiness doesn't matter. In fact, it can be quite helpful sometimes—and fun!*

I smiled. "Yeah, thanks, Dad, the cabbage was really useful."

He nodded, his eyes crinkling. "Excellent! Enjoy your day. And Bloom, do keep taking risks; as I always say, a little bit of danger keeps us all on our toes." He winked at me and I felt my face grow hot. *Did he know?*

"Oh, and I forgot to tell you," he added. "There's a new camper arriving this afternoon. I know you'll make him most welcome."

As I watched Dad stalk off into the morning sunshine, his cape billowing in the breeze, I wondered who this new kid might be.

Hopefully a regular camper who doesn't want to turn magical creatures into clothes, I thought. *Broomsticks crossed! But even if he is a little different, and messy—*I glanced at Benji—*I'm going to make sure I give him plenty of time to show his true self. Because Dad's right . . . until you peel back the layers of someone's personality, you never know what you're going to find.*

"Come on, Benji," I said, getting up from the table. "Let's go see what's happening in camp today."

Somehow, I knew that with Benji by my side, camp would be even more exciting—and unpredictable!—than usual. I couldn't wait.